Rudy's **WINDY** Christmas

For W. W. and T. T.—H. B.

For Amy and Rebecca Nelson, and all the windy sprout lovers—B. M.

Library of Congress Cataloging-in-Publication data is on file with the publisher.

Text copyright © 2014 Helen Baugh
Illustrations copyright © HarperCollins Publishers Ltd. 2014
Illustrations by Ben Mantle
Originally published in the UK by HarperCollins Children's Books in 2014 under the title *Rudey's Windy Christmas*
Published in 2015 by Albert Whitman & Company
ISBN 978-0-8075-7173-6

Printed in China
10 9 8 7 6 5 4 3 2 1 SCP 20 19 18 17 16 15

For more information about Albert Whitman & Company,
visit our web site at www.albertwhitman.com.

Rudy's WINDY Christmas

Helen Baugh & Ben Mantle

Albert Whitman & Company
Chicago, Illinois

One Christmas Eve at Santa's house
amid the ice and snow,
the Clauses shared a festive feast
before he had to go.

Mrs. Claus, who loved her sprouts,
ate each and every one,
but Santa fed his to a friend
until the last was gone.

"Bye, bye, dear!" said Santa,
lifting one more sack of toys.
"It's time for me to go and visit
all the girls and boys."

Then Santa and his reindeer friends flew up into the sky,
the sleigh secure behind them and the presents piled high.

They just got to Australia
when Dasher took a sniff.
What was that funny smell
that had a sprouty sort of whiff?

"Oh, pardon me!" said Rudy.
"But I think I've done a **pump**.
My tummy did a rumble,
then my bottom did a
trump."

The other reindeer giggled then they flew into the sky,
the sleigh secure behind them and the presents piled high.

The air was sweet for many miles,
then Dancer took a sniff.
Somewhere over China he had
smelled that **sprouty whiff!**

"Oh, deary me!" said Rudy. "Now I've done a **windy pop**.
This is a bit embarrassing. I'll do my best to stop!"

The reindeer giggled more and then they flew into the sky,
the sleigh secure behind them and the presents piled high.

For a while the air was sweet, then Prancer took a sniff.
This time it was in India he smelled that **sprouty whiff!**

"I'm sorry, boys!" said Rudy. "But I've done a booty burp. Why did I eat so many sprouts? I feel like such a twerp."

The reindeer chuckled hard
and then they flew into the sky,
the sleigh secure behind them
and the presents piled high.

The air was sweet for quite some time, then Vixen took a sniff.
Just as they reached South Africa he smelled that sprouty whiff!

"Oh, excuse me!" said Rudy.
"What a smelly, stinky fluff!
I really wish this wind would go,
I've cut the cheese enough."

The reindeer laughed and laughed and then they flew into the sky,
the sleigh secure behind them and the presents piled high.

For a while the air was sweet, then Comet took a sniff.
On landing in the UK he had smelled that sprouty whiff!

"Oh, goodness me!" said Rudy.
"Now I've done a **great big toot!**
That really was a ripper from my
poor old **bottom flute!**"

The reindeer had hysterics
then they flew into the sky,
the sleigh secure behind them
and the presents piled high.

The air was sweet for several hours,
then Cupid took a sniff.
'Cause once more (in the USA)
he smelled that **sprouty whiff!**

"Forgive me, please!" said Rudy.
"But I've blown my rear-end trumpet!
I can't believe there was enough wind
left inside to pump it!"

Donder, Blitzen, and the
other reindeer rolled around,

doubled up with laughter
as they lay upon the ground.

"They've laughed so much they're out of puff!" said Santa. "They can't fly! How ever will we get this heavy sleigh home through the sky?"

"Some super-turbo gas
is what we need now!"
Rudy boomed...

He stuck his windy bottom in the air...

and off they **ZOOMED!**

But when they reached the North Pole,
Santa got a **big** surprise...

all the elves had wrapped their
stripey scarves up to their eyes.

"We've had an awful time!"
one little elf told Santa Claus.
"Ever since you left, your wife has
air pooped without pause!"

"Ho, ho, ho!" said Santa.
"Sprouts are more fun than I knew!
I think I'll eat mine up next year
so I can join in too!"

So if you wake on Christmas night
and smell a certain stink,
just look up to the sky and give
old Santa Claus a wink!